HOWARD SAVES·A HOUND

To my pet-loving children,
Megan and Ryan
—C.L.P.

To my wife Cathy Warfel
for putting up with me,
and to my friend Ned Bustard
for giving me this opportunity.
—D.M.H.W.

ISBN# 1-930710-41-0
Copyright ©2000 Veritas Press

Veritas Press
1250 Belle Meade Drive
Lancaster, PA 17601

First edition

WRITTEN BY CARL L. PETTICOFFER
ILLUSTRATED BY DAVID M. H. WARFEL

HOWARD SAVES · A HOUND

Veritas Press

I awake as our rooster crows, and I bound out of bed. The hour is near to join Father on the hunt. My first hunt! Mother calls me. "Howard, time to eat! You must soon go!"

Before I leave the house, I eat ground flour muffins and milk, and then I run to find Father.

Outside the sky is cloudy, and the air is cold. I run to the estate of the Count. He is the ruler of our town, and his wife the Countess is kind and as pretty as a flower.

I turn left past the horse stables and find Father at the dog kennels. Father is the master of the hounds for the Count.

He grooms them and feeds them and trains them to hunt. Father shouts commands to the other men who will help him run the hounds.

We join the crowd of huntsmen who stand by the gate. "Do we hunt grouse or foxes today, Father?"

"Today we hunt fallow deer in the Forest of Dowd." The sleek brown horses are led from their food. They mow the grass as they browse by our side.

When the Count appears, all the men bow to him. The Countess stands by a window in the tower, wearing a flowing gown. The men's frowns turn to smiles when they see her.

The Count mounts his horse and waves to the Countess. I ride behind Father on his big horse. When the huntsmen blow their horns, the hounds howl.

I count the crows flying over my head, showing me how loud they can be. We follow a trail over a grassy mound and enter the forest, scouting for deer.

The beaters hit the bushes with sticks. The hounds prowl in the thicket. The bowmen get set with their bows and arrows.

Our route takes us down to the river where the hounds must cross on boats. The river is too wide and deep for the dogs to swim across. Father is the master of the dogs, so

we will ride in a boat, too. As we step into our wooden rowboat, Father says to me, "You sit in the front, in the prow." He calls a few of the dogs into our boat.

They stand with their tails wagging and looking over the side, as if they are going to jump out. They bark and make low growls at the waves.

Father rows the boat across the flowing water with slow strokes. A little snow falls from the clouds, and a cold wind blows from the south.

As we reach the other shore and Father steps from our boat, it tips and one of the hounds splashes down into the water.

I throw myself into the river to save the poor fellow from drowning, and I tow him onto the ground. I scowl, for the water is cold!

After my dousing, I sputter and pound my chest. Water spouts from my mouth. The hound shakes the water from its fur, and I stroke its snout.

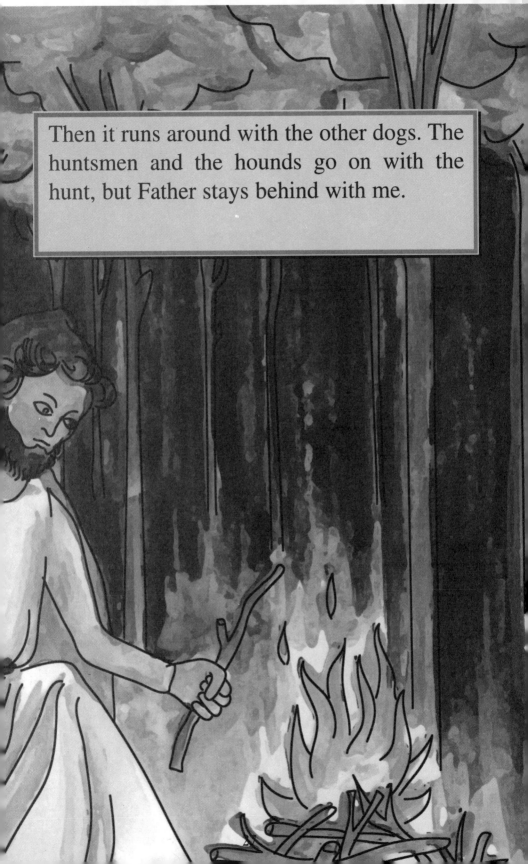

Then it runs around with the other dogs. The huntsmen and the hounds go on with the hunt, but Father stays behind with me.

With some grass and twigs he makes a fire to keep me warm. With a smile Father tells me, "Howard, the hound did not need your help. It was able to swim to dry ground.

However, I am proud of your bravery. You are no coward." As I crouch by the fire to dry my clothes, I feel drowsy.

On my first hunt I found no deer. Yet inside I am now glowing from Father's praise.